Before Jon

Isaiah Fransen

Published by Isaiah Fransen, 2023.

BEFORE JON

First edition. July 13, 2023.

ISBN: 979-8223698425

Written by Isaiah Fransen.

Table of Contents

Dedication "Book Cover Design by ebooklaunch.com"

Chapter 1 Creation
Of The Elements

ONE DAY THERE WAS A wizard named Ralph who lived in a world called the hidden world. He lived in a castle. Ralph,like all wizards, had a magic wand. Ralph had three friends ,Sophia the unicorn, Bentley the troll, and the Oatmeal warlock. Ralph the wizard invited them over to his castle for a party. When they all arrived at the castle, Ralph the wizard welcomed all of them to his castle. They were all having a good time when, all of a sudden, they heard explosions outside the castle! They looked through the castle window and there was an army of guards outside the castle! Suddenly, another wizard appeared! Ralph the wizard realized it was his evil brother, Brock the wizard! Ralph the wizard stepped outside and asked Brock the wizard, "what do you want?" Brock the wizard said, "I want your magic wand!" Ralph the wizard said, "why should I give it to you?" Brock the wizard said, "It's because I want to use it to bring back the two evil ones, so that way they can do my bidding! Then I will rule the universe!" Ralph the wizard said, "have you gone mad?" Brock the wizard said, "no I haven't!" Ralph the wizard said, "I will never give you my wand!" Then Brock the wizard said, "Okay then, I will take it by force!" Brock the wizard then said "attack!! And all his guards started attacking Ralph and his friends! Ralph the wizard said to his friends, "We are outnumbered, we must retreat!" So quickly, Ralph the wizard did a smoke screen, and by the time the smoke cleared, Ralph the wizard and his friends were gone! Then Brock the wizard was like no! "I will find you, and then that magic wand will be mine! Meanwhile, Sophia the unicorn, Bentley the troll, and The Oatmeal warlock were all wondering what they were going to do! Ralph the wizard led them to a tree and said, "this is the tree of the elements. We must use it to create the 3 elements which are water, fire and ice. To do that however, you all must combine your powers together!" So Sophia the unicorn, Bentley the troll, and the oatmeal Warlock, all combined their powers together and aimed their powers at the tree! Sure enough, the tree created three crystal elements which were water, fire, and ice. Then Ralph the wizard said to Sophia the unicorn, Bentley the troll, and the oatmeal warlock, "you must take one crystal each, and take it home with you! Guard them, and don't let each of them out of your sight!" They were all like, "okay!" Ralph the wizard said, "I must now start my journey to stop my brother from getting my magic wand and unleashing the two evil ones!" So Sophia the unicorn, Bentley the troll, and the Oatmeal warlock, all headed back to their homes with the elements. Ralph the wizard started his journey to stop his brother from getting his wand and unleashing the two evil ones!

Chapter 2 The Journey Begins

RALPH THE WIZARD STARTED his long journey to his evil brother's castle to stop him from taking his wand. On his way to the castle, he decided he would take a shortcut through the woods. He kept going deeper and deeper into the forest. All of a sudden he heard growling! Sure enough, there was a pack of wolves that had been stalking him! Now they had surrounded him, with no possible way to escape! Ralph the wizard used his magic wand to lift the wolves off the ground and throw them against the trees! This gave him time to run away! While running through the woods, Ralph the wizard came up to a pond. He could hear the wolves were coming closer, and now he needed to find a way to get across the pond! Ralph the wizard spotted an old boat with holes in it! He needed a way to plug the holes up to make it across the pond. Ralph the wizard used his magic wand to fix the boat and row across the pond to safety. Ralph the wizard got out of the boat and realized he didn't recognize this area of the forest. Shortly, he came up to a cave and decided that he should take shelter there for the night. However, Ralph the wizard woke up late that night and heard a different growl! Sure enough, it was a big huge bear and he then realized he was in a bear's cave! Ralph the wizard got up and fought the bear with his magic wand to try and escape! This angered the bear,and the bear started to attack Ralph the Wizard with his sharp claws. Eventually, Ralph the wizard used his magic wand to move the bear over to the side of the cave so he could escape! Outside the cave,the bear still chased after him! After escaping the bear, he suddenly came across a pack of hungry wolves! Fortunately,all of a sudden, Ralph the wizard heard galloping coming towards him! Sure enough, it was Sophia the unicorn coming to his rescue! Sophia the unicorn then used the water element to make it rain heavily so that the wolves and the bear had to take cover. This allowed Ralph the wizard and Sophia the unicorn to make their getaway! Sophia the unicorn said to Ralph the wizard, "what are you doing out here?!" and Ralph the wizard said "I decided I was going to take a shortcut and then I got lost". Sophia the unicorn started laughing and said "next time make sure you don't take shortcuts or I'll end up having to save you again". Sophia the unicorn and Ralph the wizard got out of the forest. However, once they both got out of the forest they were met by Brock the Wizard's army of guards. The guards started to attack Ralph the wizard and Sophia the unicorn so they could take the wand. Eventually Ralph the wizard and Sophia the unicorn managed to take out all of the guards. Ralph the wizard said to Sophia the unicorn "I must continue my journey to stop my brother", Sophia the unicorn said, "Are you sure you don't want me to come with you?" Ralph the wizard said " No, I need to do this on my own". Sophia the unicorn headed back to her home while Ralph the wizard continued his journey to stop his brother from getting his wand and unleashing the two evil ones.

Chapter 3 The Mountain Of No Return

RALPH THE WIZARD CAME up to a mountain which he had never seen before. Ralph said to himself, "I need to get past this mountain so I can stop my brother from getting my wand and releasing the two evil ones". Ralph the wizard couldn't go around the mountain because there was no way around, so he had to climb up. Ralph the wizard started to climb the mountain and managed to get to the middle of the mountain when he noticed that it was very unstable. Ralph the wizard had to be very quick and careful, otherwise there might be a rock slide which could trap him on the mountain! So, Ralph the wizard was being as careful as he could. Ralph the wizard heard something which turned out to be an army of guards following him up the mountain! Ralph the wizard had to do something to prevent the army of guards from making too much noise and causing a rock slide. Ralph the wizard ran as fast as he could away from the army of guards so he could make as much distance from them as possible. However, the army of guards kept getting closer to Ralph. Ralph the wizard quietly said to the Army of guards,

"Please be very quiet, the mountain is unstable and too much noise could cause a rock slide." The army of guards yelled, "why should we care?!" Then suddenly the rocks started to come down and the army of guards screamed "Oh no!" The guards ran back down the mountain as quickly as they could! However, Ralph the wizard needed to get to the other side of the mountain. It was so unstable that the rocks started coming from every direction. Ralph the wizard was helpless and in great danger! Just in time, Bentley the troll came to his rescue and started holding the rocks back while Ralph the wizard made his way back up the mountain. Ralph the wizard made it to the top, however, Bentley the troll was still holding the rocks, so Ralph the wizard had to do something! Ralph the wizard used his magic wand to get the rocks off Bentley the troll. Ralph the wizard and Bentley the troll then made their way down the other side of the mountain. However, the rocks were still coming down the mountain! Ralph the wizard told Bentley the troll to use the fire element to blast the rocks with the fire. Bentley the troll used the fire element and blasted fire towards the rocks! The fire held back the rocks so they could make their escape! Ralph the wizard ran further down the mountain while Bentley the troll stopped using the fire element and ran as fast as he could down the mountain! Just in time! The whole mountain basically collapsed, and Ralph the wizard said "I will definitely not be going back this way!" Bentley the troll asked, "What were you doing on the mountain of no return? They call it that for a reason!" Ralph the wizard said, "there was no way around the mountain, so I decided to go up the mountain". Bentley the troll said "There was another way you could have gone. You could have gone up the volcano where I live." Bentley the troll was shaking his head in disapproval and said, "I am headed back home, are you coming with me?" Ralph the wizard said, "No, I have to continue my journey to stop my brother Brock from taking my magic wand and unleashing the two evil ones." Bentley the troll said, "Okay, well don't get yourself in any more trouble". Bentley the troll headed home while Ralph the wizard continued his journey to stop his brother Brock from taking his wand and unleashing the two evil ones.

Chapter 4 The Fire Monster

RALPH THE WIZARD CAME up to what appeared to be a lava lake. He had to find a way across it. However, Just then, Ralph the wizard noticed something emerging from the lava lake. To his surprise it was a Fire Monster! The Fire Monster started to throw fireballs at Ralph the wizard. Ralph the wizard had to dodge all the fireballs that were being thrown at him by the Fire Monster! Ralph the wizard then used his magic wand against the Fire Monster! The magic wand was no match for the Fire Monster! Suddenly, the Oatmeal warlock appeared and started to use his powers against the Fire Monster! But still, that was not working! Then Ralph the wizard had an idea. He told the Oatmeal warlock to use the ice element against the Fire Monster. The Oatmeal warlock used the ice element against the Fire monster. Sure enough, the Fire Monster was frozen solid! Then the Oatmeal warlock asked Ralph the wizard what he was doing out by the lava lake. Ralph the wizard said, "I am on my journey to stop my brother Brock the wizard from taking my magic wand and unleashing the two evil ones." Then the Oatmeal warlock said, "We have to get you across this lava lake somehow." Ralph the wizard had an idea, "Why don't we use the ice element to freeze the lava lake so I can get across safely?" So the Oatmeal warlock used the ice element to freeze the lava lake. Ralph the wizard started across the lava lake and made it to the other side. The Oatmeal warlock asked, "Are you sure you don't want me to come along?" Ralph the wizard said, "No,I need to do this on my own." So the Oatmeal warlock said, "Okay, but don't get into any more trouble!" So the Oatmeal warlock headed back home, and Ralph the wizard continued his journey to stop his brother Brock from taking his wand and unleashing the two evil ones. Meanwhile, one of the guards headed back to Brock the Wizard's Castle and told Brock the wizard that his brother Ralph the wizard was on his way to his castle. Brock the wizard said, "Good let him come! I'm going to have a little surprise for him!" Meanwhile, Ralph the wizard came up to what appeared to be a desert. Suddenly he saw in the distance what appeared to be a pyramid. He thought he should take shelter in the pyramid for the night. He went inside and saw it was pitch black. So, Ralph the Wizard lit a stick on fire and went deeper into the pyramid. Eventually he came to a dead end! He said to himself, "Now what?" All of a sudden he fell through a trap door and landed in another room inside the pyramid! He got up and said, "where am I?" It was a room full of ancient artifacts. Suddenly, the trap door closed above him and he was completely trapped deep inside the pyramid! He had nowhere else to go but deeper into the pyramid! Ralph the wizard started to go deeper into the pyramid to find a way out!

Chapter 5 The Mummy's Tomb

RALPH THE WIZARD ENDED up in what appeared to be another chamber inside the pyramid. He noticed something in the distance! Suddenly, a live mummy was coming right towards him! Ralph said to himself, "Oh no, what am I going to do!?" And he started to run away from the mummy! Ralph the wizard was running away from the mummy when he came to a dead end with a pit full of snakes! The mummy was getting closer and closer to Ralph the wizard! Ralph the wizard had to do something! He remembered that he had his magic wand and he tried to use it against the mummy! Unfortunately, the magic wand wasn't working against the mummy! Now he had to find a way across the snake pit without falling into it! Ralph the wizard saw an old piece of rope. He had an idea to use his magic wand to attach the rope to the ceiling so he could swing across to the other side of the snake pit! So, quickly, Ralph the wizard grabbed onto the rope and swung across the snake pit and escaped the mummy! However, Ralph the wizard still needed to find a way out of the pyramid. He found another stick and lit it on fire to find his way out of the pyramid. Ralph the wizard started to walk along the halls of the pyramid to find a way out and eventually saw a little bit of light up ahead. Ralph the wizard finally found what appeared to be a door and got himself out of the pyramid. However, when Ralph the wizard got out of the pyramid there was a sandstorm outside! Ralph the wizard started walking through the sandstorm. He continued walking until he came up to what appeared to be an oasis in the middle of the desert. Ralph the wizard yelled "Yes! Water!" and grabbed some water from the oasis, however, when he tried to drink it, it was sand! Ralph the wizard said "Oh no! I must have fallen for a mirage! I must have been getting really thirsty!" Ralph the wizard then saw what appeared to be a village in the distance. He decided to walk towards the village to get some water. Ralph the wizard got to the village and realized that this village was full of bad guys. The bad guys saw Ralph the wizard standing just outside the village. Ralph the wizard started to run in the opposite direction to avoid the bad guys! However, he was quickly captured and taken back to the bad guy's village! Ralph the wizard was thrown into a jail cell by the bad guys. The bad guys said to each other "Hooray! Now we can take him to Brock the wizard's castle and get our bounty for capturing him!" Ralph the wizard thought to himself, "That's where I need to go", so he had a plan to cooperate with the bad guys to get to Brock the wizard's castle. The bad guys loaded Ralph the wizard into a carriage and they took off to Brock the wizard's castle.

Chapter 6 Entering Brock The Wizard's Castle

RALPH THE WIZARD AND the bad guys were heading towards Brock the wizard's castle. Meanwhile, Ralph the wizard was planning in his head what he was going to do once he got to his brother's castle. The carriage rolled up the castle gates and was let in by the guards. The bad guys were instructed to bring Ralph the wizard to Brock the wizard. The bad guys brought Ralph the wizard to Brock the wizard and demanded their bounty be paid in full. Brock the wizard said, "Forget it, throw them in the dungeon!" Ralph the wizard said, "We finally meet again, my brother!" Brock the wizard said, "Give me your wand and I may decide to spare you from my dungeon." Ralph the wizard said "Never, I can't let you unleash the two evil ones!" Brock the wizard said, "Well I have a little surprise for you!" Sure enough, Brock the wizard brought Sophia the unicorn, Bentley the troll, and the oatmeal warlock into the throne room. Brock the wizard said "I will give you one last chance to give me the wand or your friends will pay the price". Ralph the wizard finally said "I guess I have no choice but to give you the wand, as long as you spare my friends". The three friends yelled out "No! Don't do it!" Ralph the wizard said "Well, I can't let him hurt you guys. You've saved me one too many times!" Ralph the wizard gave Brock the wizard his wand. Brock the wizard said, " Finally, now I have his wand and I will be able to go to the cave and unleash the two evil ones!" Brock the wizard instructed the guards to get his carriage and take Ralph the wizard and his friends to the dungeon and lock them up. Ralph the wizard and his friends could see no way out of the dungeon but wondered what they could do to get out of there. Ralph the wizard remembered that even though he didn't have his wand, they still had the three elements which Brock the wizard didn't know about. Sophia the unicorn, Bentley the troll and the Oatmeal warlock used all of the elements against the gate to break out of the dungeon. The guards saw what happened and yelled, "Get them, before they escape!" Ralph the wizard and his three friends managed to take out the guards one by one! Ralph the wizard said, "We must stop my brother from using the wand and unleashing the two evil ones". So, the group took off from Brock the wizard's castle and started the journey together to stop him from unleashing the two evil ones. Meanwhile, Brock the wizard was riding in his carriage when one of his guards ran up and told him that Ralph the wizard and his friends had escaped from the dungeon. Brock the wizard said "We must get them back into the dungeon so they won't interfere with the plan! I want all guards on high alert and I want them captured immediately!" Brock the wizard said, "Alert all the neighboring villages to keep a look out for the prisoners and offer them a large bounty for capturing them". Meanwhile, Ralph the wizard and his friends came up to another village wanting to get a drink of water. The villagers saw Ralph the wizard and his friends coming into their village. Suddenly,an angry mob of villagers surrounded them. Ralph the wizard was shocked and realized his brother, Brock the wizard must have alerted the neighboring villages of their escape! Ralph the wizard and his friends thought to themselves, "Oh no, what are we going to do?"

Chapter 7 Escaping The Angry Mob

RALPH THE WIZARD AND his friends needed to devise a plan to escape the mob without hurting the villagers. Ralph said to the villagers, "Do you really trust my brother to pay the bounty for our capture? Last time the villagers that brought me to my brother were put in jail. My brother is on his way to a cave to unleash the two evil ones to destroy us all! Maybe you should let us go to stop him?" The villagers whispered amongst themselves before making their decision. The villagers said, "Fine, we'll let you go!" Meanwhile, Brock the wizard heard that the villagers had betrayed him and said "They what?! We're going to make a little stop in the village and make sure they pay the price for letting them go!" Meanwhile, Ralph the wizard and his friends were getting water in the village. They then found an Inn to stay the night before continuing their journey the next day to stop his brother. Ralph the wizard and his friends checked into the Inn and they all went to sleep. However, in the middle of the night, they heard something outside. Ralph the wizard woke up and saw his brother terrorizing the villagers. Ralph the wizard and his friends went downstairs immediately to help the villagers and stop his brother. Brock the wizard came out of his carriage and said to his guards "Attack!". Ralph the wizard and his friends started to attack the guards but they were outnumbered. Ralph the wizard and his friends had no choice but to pull out the elements. Brock the wizard yelled "Where did you get those?!" Ralph the wizard said "We created them in case of an emergency just like this!" Brock the wizard said "That doesn't matter I will still be victorious". Then, Brock the wizard headed back to his guards. Then his guards lit the village on fire!! Ralph the wizard said to his friends "we have to rescue the villagers quickly and get them to safety!" Ralph the wizard and his friends split up and rescued the villagers. Sophia the unicorn went back to the burning hotel! The hotel clerk was in danger as the hotel was about to collapse on top of her! Sophia the unicorn galloped up and yelled to the hotel clerk, "Hop on,before the building collapses!"The hotel clerk hopped onto her back, and Sophia the unicorn brought her to safety. Meanwhile,Bentley the troll headed to the orphanage and saw that children were trying to escape but couldn't find a way out! Bentley the troll decided to break through one of the walls of the orphanage, and said to the children,"Follow me!" They all escaped one by one! The Oatmeal warlock saw a family trapped inside their house and went in to rescue them! One of the family members was stuck underneath a collapsed support beam.The oatmeal warlock had to do something! He lifted the burning support beam off the family member while another family member helped on the other side.They got him out! Meanwhile, Ralph the wizard decided he was going to go after his brother! Brock the wizard was about to leave the village in his carriage when Ralph the wizard caught up to him and was furious! and said, "what have you done to innocent villagers?" Brock the wizard said, "Why should I care? I am going to be the ruler of the universe soon!" Ralph the wizard said to Brock the wizard,"I challenge you to come fight me and we will see who's the true victor!" Brock the wizard said, "You are on!"

Chapter 8 Showdown

BROCK THE WIZARD SAID, "How are you supposed to fight me when you have no wand?" Ralph the wizard said, "Because we have the elements!" Then his friends came and stood by Ralph the wizard. His friends said, "We have your back Ralph!" Brock the wizard said,"Fine, then I will use my magic wand and your magic wand together!" Brock the wizard was very powerful and dangerous with two wands together! Nevertheless,Sophia the unicorn, Bentley the troll, and the Oatmeal warlock said "Bring it on!" They used the three elements against Brock the wizard. Brock the wizard deflected their power with his two magic wands and blasted them back. The friends dodged the attack and said, "We have to get more power somehow!" All of a sudden, there was a big storm. Ralph the wizard noticed that there was a fourth element that came down from the sky. Ralph the wizard said, "We must use this element and all the other elements together!" Ralph the wizard retrieved the element from the sky and to his surprise it contained the lightning element! Brock the wizard said "How did that appear? Now you must pay!" Brock the wizard used the two magic wands to blast them one more time! Sohpia the unicorn, Bentley the troll, the Oatmeal warlock, and Ralph the wizard used their four elements at the same time to attack Brock the wizard! Sure enough, Brock the wizard was flat on the ground from the joint attack. Sohpia the unicorn, Bentley the troll, the Oatmeal warlock, and Ralph the wizard said, "You have been defeated!" Ralph the wizard said, "Give me back the wand!" Brock the wizard quickly got back onto his feet with the two wands in hand and said, "Never!" He then got into his carriage to flee. Ralph the wizard and his friends went back to the village. Sophia the unicorn used her water element to put out the fire. All of the villagers were so grateful and said, "You guys are the best!" Ralph the wizard said, "We must be going now, but good luck!" Meanwhile, Brock the wizard was on his way to the cave and thought to himself, "How am I going to stop my brother from stopping me?" Suddenly,he came up with a terrible idea. He would ask Rodney the giant to capture Ralph the wizard and his friends and bring them back to his castle and eat them for lunch! Meanwhile, Ralph the wizard and his friends continued on their way to stop Brock the wizard from unleashing the two evil ones. Suddenly, the ground was shaking and they noticed there was a giant coming towards them! Ralph the wizard told his friends to run, but it was too late! The giant picked them up! Ralph the wizard said, "Who are you?" The giant said, "My name is Rodney the giant and I was ordered by Brock the wizard to take you back to my castle and eat you for lunch!" Ralph the wizard was shocked and said, "Oh no! What are we going to do now?" Rodney the giant took them back to his castle and put them in a cage and started preparing a pot. Ralph the wizard and his friends quickly realized that they had to get out of there somehow!

Chapter 9 Finding A Way Out Of Rodney The Giant's Castle

RALPH THE WIZARD AND his friends needed to find a way out of Rodney the Giants castle without Rodney the giant noticing! So Sophia the unicorn, Bentley the troll, and The Oatmeal the warlock, and Ralph the wizard tried using the elements to break out of the cage! However it wasn't working! Then Ralph the wizard had an idea! He had a paperclip in his pocket that he was going to use it to pick the lock of the cage. Ralph the wizard hopped on Sophia the unicorn's back and managed to pick the lock and to open the cage! They quickly got out of the cage and started to tiptoe slowly away so that the giant didn't notice them! However, Sophia the unicorn accidentally made too much noise and Rodney the giant saw them! He said, "Where do you think you're going?" Ralph the wizard yelled "Run!" So Ralph the wizard and his friends started running around the castle to get away from Rodney the giant! Just then, Sophia the unicorn saw what appeared to be a supply closet. She yelled to everyone, "Quick, in here!" so everyone ran into the supply closet! Rodney the giant was like, "where did they go?"

He walked right past the closet! Ralph the wizard whispered, "We need to find a way out of here now before Rodney the giant comes back." Bentley the troll noticed that there was a huge window across the room. They quickly ran across the room to the window. However, the window was too high for them to reach! Ralph the wizard saw a rope in the supply closet. Ralph the wizard quickly ran back to the supply closet to grab the rope. He then hopped on one of his friend's back to get up to the window. He then used the rope to pull up his friends to the window. However Sophia the unicorn could not climb the rope because she was a horse and couldn't hold on! Ralph the wizard had to think of something! He had an idea! He sent the Oatmeal warlock and Bentley the troll back down and tied the Rope around Sophia the unicorn. Then they went back up to the window edge and pulled really hard. They brought Sophia the unicorn up to the window edge. They then realized that the window was too high up from the ground for them to jump down! Ralph the wizard said, "We're going to have to use the rope to lower us down one at a time!" So Ralph the wizard attached the rope to the edge of the window. Ralph the wizard went first and made it down to the bottom. Bentley the troll went second and made it to the bottom. Then the oatmeal warlock went third and made it to the bottom. Then Ralph the wizard said to Sophia the unicorn, "Why aren't you coming down?" Sophia the Unicorn said, "I can't because I'm a horse!" "I forgot about that," said Ralph the wizard. Suddenly, Rodney the giant saw Sophia the unicorn on the window ledge! Ralph the wizard said to Sophia the Unicorn, "Hurry, you have to jump!" Sophia the Unicorn said, "Are you crazy!" Ralph the wizard said, "Don't worry, we will catch you!" So Sophia the Unicorn made a leap of faith and jumped from the window edge! Ralph the wizard and his friends caught her just in time and they escaped! Rodney the giant yelled, "I will get you guys one day and I will eat you for lunch!" Meanwhile, Brock the wizard was on his way to the cave where the two evil ones were. One of his guards said, "We are almost there!" Brock the wizard was like, "Good, soon I will unleash the two evil ones and they will do my bidding and I will rule the universe!"

Chapter 10 The Cave

BROCK THE WIZARD AND his guards made it to the cave which was surrounded by lava. Brock the wizard said to his guards, "Find another way around this lava, now!" The guards were like, "Yes sir!" Just then, Ralph the wizard, Sophia the unicorn, Bentley the troll,and the Oatmeal warlock arrived at the cave and saw Brock the wizard and his guards there. Brock the wizard was like, "How did you escape Rodney the Giant?" Ralph the wizard said, "never mind that, give me my magic wand back now!" Brock the wizard said, "Never!" Then Brock the wizard used both his and Ralph the Wizard's magic wand to attack Ralph the wizard and his friends! Ralph the wizard and his friends used the elements to fight back! Eventually they knocked Brock the wizard down to his knees! Ralph the wizard and his friends went over to Brock the wizard and Ralph the wizard said, "There is nowhere to run! Now give me my magic wand back!" Brock the wizard said, "Never!" He said to his guards, "Seize them!" So the guards started to fight Ralph the wizard and his friends! Ralph the wizard and his friends tried to fight back, however, there were too many of them! They were captured and taken hostage! Brock the wizard yelled, "Grab the elements!" Ralph the wizard and his friends were like, "No!" However, it was too late and Brock the wizard now had Ralph the wizard's magic wand and all four elements! Brock the wizard was like, "Yes!" Now I have even more power!" Ralph the wizard said, "You won't get away with this!" Brock the wizard replied, "I already have, and there's nothing you can do to stop me!" Brock the wizard then used the ice element to freeze the lava temporarily so they could get across to the cave. Brock the wizard and some of his guards crossed over the frozen lava and got to the other side where the cave was. However, the other half the guards were wondering what to do with Ralph the wizard and his friends. Brock the wizard said,"Bring them along, as I would like them to see me unleash the two evil ones so I can rule the universe!" So the guards said to Ralph the wizard and his friends, "Alright you guys, move it!" So they went across the frozen lava to the other side where the cave was. Ralph the wizard's friends whispered to Ralph the wizard, "What are we going to do?" Ralph the wizard whispered back to his friends, "Let's play along for now." Brock the wizard and his guards and everyone else were ready to enter the cave. It was very dark, so Brock the wizard told his guards to light his lantern. They lit the lantern and they kept moving deeper into the cave. Suddenly they heard something! It was a swarm of bats! Brock the wizard yelled, "Everyone run!" Brock the wizard and his guards and everyone ran away from the swarm of bats! They eventually got deeper into the cave and got away from the swarm of bats! They came across what appeared to be an underground lake. Brock the wizard said to his guards,"Find a way to get us across this underground lake, now!" The guards said, "Yes sir!"

Chapter 11 Finding A Way Across The Underground Lake

BROCK THE WIZARD AND his guards were building a boat to get across the underground lake. It was quite the task and it took a very long time to build it, but it was finally finished! Brock the wizard boarded the boat first, followed by his guards, then Ralph the wizard and his friends. They took off in the boat to get to the other side of the underground lake. Without warning a pack of crocodiles appeared! They were swimming right towards them! Brock the wizard said to his guards, "do something!" The crocodiles got to the boat and started chomping on it! Brock the wizard and everyone were screaming that they were going to sink and get eaten by the crocodiles! Just then, one of the guards remembered that he had a sandwich in his pocket! He tossed it into the water and the crocodiles went after it! Brock the wizard said to his guards, "Move it, before they come back!" The guards were like, "Yes sir!"So they kept rowing as fast as they could! However,something very big started coming towards them! Brock the wizard yelled, "What now!" To their surprise, it was a lake monster! Brock the wizard yelled to his guards again. "Get us out of here!" So they started to row across the lake at lightning speed trying to get away from the lake monster! However, the lake monster was catching up to them and started to breathe fire towards them! Brock the wizard was yelling to his guards, "Can't you guys go any faster?" His guards said, "We're going as fast as we can!" So Brock the wizard had to take matters into his own hands! He used his magic wand, and Ralph the wizards magic wand against the lake monster. Unfortunately they weren't working, and this got the lake monster even more angry! The lake monster started going underneath the boat, trying to capsize it! Then Brock the wizard said to his guards, "Hurry up and row faster!" Luckily they were almost to the shore! However, the lake monster started to breathe fire again, right at them! Brock the wizard used the water element to deflect the fire away from the boat ! They made it across just in time and the lake monster went back underwater! Brock the wizard got off the boat first, followed by his guards and Ralph the wizard and his friends. The guards said to Ralph the wizard and his friends, "Keep moving!" There was a cave and they started deeper into the cave! Eventually they came to a part of the cave which was full of ice and was very slippery. Brock the wizard's guards said to Brock the wizard, "Be careful as it's very slippery!" Brock the wizard was like, "Who cares? Keep moving!" However when Brock the wizard stepped on to the ice he started to slip and slide everywhere! Brock the Wizard's guards yelled,"Hold on sir! We will save you!" However, when they tried to save him, they were all slipping and sliding everywhere as well! Brock the wizard yelled, "You fools, help me!" Brock the wizard's guards said, "We are trying!" Suddenly, Brock the wizard bumped into something! To his surprise it was an ice monster! Brock the wizard yelled to his guards, "You fools, do something!"

Chapter 12 The Ice Monster

BROCK THE WIZARD AND his guards and Ralph and his friends, were face to face with a giant ice monster! Brock the wizard yelled to his guards again, "Hurry up and do something!" So the guards started to attack the ice monster! However, they were getting nowhere as the ice monster was too powerful! So Brock the wizard yelled to his guards, "Fall back," as the ice monster was even more angry! It started blowing frost at them, trying to freeze them! Then the ice monster started to break the ice so icicles would fall on top of them! Brock the wizard yelled again to his guards, "Attack the ice monster!" However, the ice monster was getting even angrier and started to take out all the guards with his icy hands! Finally, Brock the wizard had enough! He decided to use both his, and Ralph the wizard's magic wand against the ice monster! However, even that wasn't working! Then the ice monster started to charge Brock the wizard! As one last line of defense Brock The Wizard used the fire element against the ice monster! The fire element melted him until he was nothing but a puddle on the ground! Brock the wizard said to his guards, "Hurry up you fools keep moving!" The other half of the guards said to Ralph the wizard and his friends, "You heard him, keep moving!" They all ended up going deeper into the cave and eventually they came up to what appeared to be a statue of a dragon and crow! Brock the wizard said, "I have finally found it! Now I can unleash the two evil ones and they will do my bidding and I will rule the universe!" Finally,with all their strength, Ralph the wizard, Sophia the unicorn, Bentley the troll, and the Oatmeal warlock took out the guards that were holding them hostage! Ralph the wizard said, "This is the end of the line for you Brock!" Then Brock the wizard said to the rest of his guards, "You fools, get them!" The guards started to fight Ralph and his friends but Ralph and his friends were gaining the upper hand! Brock the wizard said to himself. "I've had enough of this, it's time for me to unleash my full power! So Brock the wizard used his and Ralph the wizard's magic wand and combined them into one wand! Brock the wizard started to grow gigantic! Then he used the 4 elements and all 4 elements started floating around him making him invincible! Brock the wizard then said to Ralph the wizard, "What are you going to do now Ralph the wizard, as I'm more powerful than you and all your friends combined!" Ralph the wizard said,no you're not! You may be more powerful than me and my friends right now, but that power will eventually betray you!" Brock the wizard then said,"What are you talking about! I'm the most powerful wizard in the universe and I will be even more powerful once I unleash the two evil ones!" Ralph the wizard said, "I'm afraid I can't let you do that!" Then Sophia the unicorn, Bentley the troll and the Oatmeal warlock said to Ralph the wizard, "We are with you until the very end!" Ralph the wizard said, "Thank you guys, you are the best friends that a wizard could ever ask for!" Are you guys ready?" They all said,"Yes!" Then Ralph the wizard said to his friends, "Are you really ready? This will be our ultimate battle! Remember the whole universe is counting on us!" Brock the wizard said, "How in the world are you thinking you're going to stop me as I'm more powerful than all of you now! I will destroy you all!"

Chapter 13 The Final Battle Between Ralph And Brock The Wizard

BROCK THE WIZARD STARTED to use all his attack methods against them. He used his magic wand and began to blast them with it! Ralph the wizard and his friends managed to dodge those forceful attacks! Next, Brock the wizards guards started attacking them! Sophia the unicorn, Bentley the troll, and the Oatmeal warlock said to Ralph the wizard, "We will take care of the guards, you must go and stop your brother!" So Ralph the wizard had to quickly come up with a plan to stop his brother! He didn't seem to have any way to stop him! He needed to get the wand back from Brock! That would involve a strategic distraction! Finally,Sophia the unicorn, Bentley the troll, And The Oatmeal Warlock finished taking out all the guards! Ralph the wizard said to his friends, "Can you distract Brock for me while I try to retrieve the wand?" His friends said, "Yes we sure can!" So all his friends all attacked Brock the wizard. Brock the wizard yelled, "You can't defeat me! I'll tell you once again, I'm more powerful than all of you combined!" Suddenly, Brock the wizard noticed that Ralph the wizard wasn't there! He realized it was a distraction! Sure enough, Ralph the wizard climbed up on Brock the Wizards back and started to go for the wand! Brock the wizard screamed, "Oh no you don't! I'm going to squash you like a bug!" Somehow,Ralph the wizard managed to get to the wand and knocked it out and Brock the Wizard's hands! Brock the wizard was like, "Oh no, I must have the wand!" So then both Brock the wizard and Ralph the wizard raced towards the wand! Ralph the wizard got to it first! Ralph the wizard said, "This is the end of the line for you!" Brock the wizard said, "You're wrong! I still have the 4 elements!" So he decided to use the water element to flood the cave! Ralph the wizard said to his friends, "You guys have to get out of here! I will deal with Brock the wizard myself!" His friends said, 'No,we are with each other until the very end!" Ralph the wizard said, "Thanks, you guys are awesome!" Then Ralph the wizard started to use his magic wand against Brock the wizard! He managed to knock the water element right out of his hand! Brock the wizard was like, "No, I cannot be defeated!" Ralph the wizard told Sophia the Unicorn to go grab the water element and so she grabbed it. Brock the wizard said, "You may have gotten the water element, but I still have 3 of the elements left!" So Brock the wizard started using the fire element against them! But Sophia the Unicorn was like, "Oh yeah, I have the water element!" Sophia the Unicorn used the water element against the fire element! Once again, it knocked the fire element right out of Brock the wizard's hands! Ralph the wizard yelled to Bentley the troll,

"Grab the fire element!" Quickly, Bentley the troll grabbed the fire element! Brock the wizard yelled,"No, not again! But I still have 2 of the elements left! So now Brock the wizard used the ice element against them! Bentley the troll yelled, "Oh yeah! I have the fire element!" So Bentley the troll used the fire element against the ice element and again knocked it out of Brock the wizard's hands! Ralph the wizard said to the Oatmeal warlock, "Grab the ice element!" Quickly as he could the Oatmeal warlock grabbed the ice element! Brock the wizard screamed, 'No, how is this possible! How is it that I only have 1 element left?" Now he started using the lightning element against them! The Oatmeal warlock said, "Oh yeah! I have the ice element!" Ralph the wizard yelled to the Oatmeal warlock, "No!" However it was too late! The oatmeal warlock was using the ice element against the lightning element! However Brock the wizard was gaining the upper hand! The Oatmeal warlock was like, "Oh no!" Then he realized ice and lightning don't mix! Sure enough, the Oatmeal warlock ended up getting blasted by Brock the wizard's lightning element! Everyone was rushing over to the Oatmeal warlock to make sure he was all right! He said "I am, but that was a close one!" The Oatmeal warlock asked, "How are we going to get the lightning element away from him?" Ralph the wizard said, "There is only one way, and that is to destroy the lightning element! Ralph the wizard's friends said, "Are you sure you want to do that?" Ralph the wizard said, "I'm afraid there's no other way!" So Ralph the wizard used his magic wand to do one big blast against the lightning element and his brother Brock the wizard! Sure enough the blast got through and completely destroyed the lightning element! Brock the wizard was like, "This is impossible! I cannot be defeated!" But sure enough, he started to shrink back down to his original size! Ralph the wizard yelled, "It's over Brock the wizard!" Brock the wizard yelled back, "Are you sure about that?" Out of nowhere, one of Brock the wizards guards took Ralph the wizard's wand right out of his hands and gave it to Brock the wizard! Brock the wizard screamed, "Finally, I will unleash the two evil ones!" So Brock the wizard used the magic wand against the statue of the Dragon and Crow! Ralph the wizard yelled to his friends, "Stop him!" But it was too late! The statue started to crack and Brock the wizard yelled "Finally, I have unleashed the two evil ones!" Sure enough Carey the dragon broke free along with her crow named Doug! They were like, "We are free at last!" Brock the wizard yelled, "Yes I've freed you, now you will serve me and I will rule the universe!" They asked, "Who was it that said that you are going to rule the universe?" Brock the wizard asked, "What do you mean?" They laughed and said, "You really thought that you were going to rule the universe? You are wrong! We are going to rule the universe and not you!" Brock the wizard yelled to his guards, "Do something!" However it was too late! Carey the dragon grabbed the wand from Brock the wizard and he said. "Finally we have the wand after all these years!" Brock the wizard and his guards tried to fight back however, Carey the dragon opened up a portal and they all got sucked in! Including Brock the wizard! The portal closed and they were never to be seen again! However Ralph the wizard and his friends were still there, and now they had a whole new problem on their hands!

Chapter 14 The Two Evil Ones Unleashed

CAREY THE DRAGON AND Doug the crow now had Ralph the wizards magic wand! Ralph the wizard and his friends were wondering what they were going to do. Then, Carey the dragon and Doug the crow said to Ralph the wizard and his friends "Now I will destroy the universe, and this other dimension called earth". Ralph the wizard and his friends asked "what is this earth you speak of?" Carcy the dragon and Doug the crow said "it is the home of the chosen one and we must destroy it before we can take over the universe, as he is a threat to our plans". Ralph the wizard said "You won't get away with this!" Then, Carey the dragon and Doug the crow started blasting Ralph the wizard and his friends with the magic wand. Ralph the wizard and his friends tried to use the remaining three elements against Carey the dragon and Doug the crow! The elements started to work against them. However, they quickly failed and Carey and dragon and Doug the crow said, "where did you get those elements?" We must destroy the elements at all costs so the chosen one does not use them to defeat us!" Then Ralph the wizard and his friends realized that the elements were very important, but they still needed to find a way to get the magic wand away from Carey the dragon and Doug the crow. Ralph the wizard asked his friends to distract Carey the dragon and Doug the crow while he tried to get his wand back. His friends said "yes we will distract them." Ralph the wizard's friends started to distract them by fighting them. Ralph the wizard needed to find a way around the fight to get the wand. So, Ralph the wizard started to sneak behind rocks while all the fighting was going on and slowly made his way behind Carey the dragon. Then, Carey the dragon and Doug the crow realized that Ralph the wizard was not with his friends. Doug the crow saw Ralph the wizard climbing up Carey the dragon's tail! Carey the dragon started wagging her tail to get Ralph the wizard off of her. However, Ralph the wizard was still holding on tight. Ralph the wizard managed to get the wand out of Carey the dragon's hands! Carey the dragon yelled "Oh no, my wand!". Carey the dragon was breathing fire as Ralph the wizard was grabbing the wand! Doug the crow tried to swoop in and grab the wand however, Ralph the wizard's friends loosened Doug the crows grip on the wand. Doug the crow finally lost his grip of the wand as Sophia the unicorn grabbed the wand from his claws. Ralph the wizard managed to grab the wand and said to Carey the dragon and Doug the crow, "this will be the end of the line for the both of you!" Carey the dragon used her fire breath against Ralph the wizard and Ralph the wizard used his magic wand against Carey the dragon. Carey the dragon yelled out "Oh no!". Ralph the wizard told his friends to use their elements and he would use his wand against Carey the dragon and Doug the crow at the same time. Ralph the wizard and his friends used all three elements and the wand against Carey the dragon and Doug the crow. However, it did not work and Carey the dragon and Doug the crow said "only the chosen one can defeat us". Then, Carey the dragon used her fire breath and half the cave started to collapse! Carey the dragon and Doug the crow flew out of the cave! Ralph the wizard and his friends were still deep in the cave, and said to one another, "We have to get out of here!" So they started to run as fast as they could! They came up to the icy cave where the ice monster was, and started to run back across the ice! But they were slipping and sliding in every direction. Ralph the wizard and his friends eventually made it across. Then, they got back to the underground lake and saw that the cave was still crumbling down! They got back into the boat that they were on before, and started to row across the lake. Then the lake monster started to chase them while Ralph and his friends were rowing as fast as they could. While the cave was collapsing the crocodiles joined the chase and started to chomp on the boat! Ralph the wizard said, "We have to get across faster". Finally, they made it across the lake and the lake monster went back into the water and the crocodiles left! Ralph the wizard and his friends got out just in time as part of the cave collapsed behind them. However, some of the cave was still stable and Carey the dragon and Doug the crow were waiting for them. Carey the dragon and Doug the crow said, "How did you make it out?" Ralph the wizard and his friends said, "Teamwork!" Carey the dragon and Doug the crow said, "We will have to finish you off ourselves!" Carey the dragon breathed fire at them again, and tried to grab Ralph the wizard's magic wand back. Ralph the wizard yelled, "You will not get my magic wand!" He started to blast Carey the dragon with his magic wand! Carey the dragon yelled, "Ouch, that hurt!" but kept breathing fire at them! However, Ralph the wizard deflected her attacks. Suddenly, Doug the crow swooped in and grabbed the magic wand from Ralph the wizard and gave it to Carey the dragon! Carey the dragon said, "Finally I have the magic wand again, now I will destroy the chosen one's world and rule the universe!" Ralph the wizard and his friends said, "No, we can't let you do that!" Ralph the wizard hopped onto Sophia the unicorn's back and started to charge Carey the dragon and Doug the crow! Sophia the unicorn with Ralph the wizard on her back crashed into Carey the dragon forcefully and made her drop the wand! Carey the dragon and Doug the crow yelled, "No!!" Ralph the wizard got his magic wand back and teleported himself and his friends back to Ralph the wizard's castle! Ralph the wizard said to his friends, "You must take the remaining elements back home with you and guard them, while I find the chosen one before it's too late". Ralph the wizard said, "When the chosen one comes to retrieve the elements, put him through some sort of test to make sure he is worthy". Ralph the wizard's friends headed back to their homes with the elements and Ralph the wizard said, "I need to find out who the chosen one is to save the universe". So, Ralph the wizard went to his library to do some research and to find out who the chosen one was.

Chapter 15 The Chosen One

RALPH THE WIZARD WAS looking through his library to see if he could find a book that would tell him about the chosen one. However, he had no luck so far. Then Ralph the wizard noticed a book on the top shelf of his library. He had no way to reach the book because it was so high up. He needed to find a way to get the book. He remembered that he had a ladder in the supply closet in his workshop. Ralph the wizard headed to his workshop and grabbed the ladder from the supply closet and brought it back up to the library to grab the book. Sure enough, Ralph the wizard got the book from the top shelf. He opened up the book and found out that there was a person from another dimension called earth. This person had used the elements to defeat Carey the dragon and Doug the crow and turned them into stone. The book didn't say who this person was and whether this person was still alive. However, the book did say, if Carey the dragon and Doug the crow were ever unleashed again that a descendent of the chosen one would defeat them. Ralph the wizard realized that the original chosen one must not be alive anymore. So, Ralph the wizard needed to look through his crystal ball and see who the chosen one was. Meanwhile, Carey the dragon and Doug the crow were trying to figure out how to get the magic wand back from Ralph the wizard. Doug the crow said that he would go grab it himself personally, and he took off to grab the magic wand. Meanwhile, back at Ralph the wizard's castle, Ralph the wizard started to look through his crystal ball to see if he could find the chosen one. However, he was having no luck in finding the chosen one. Ralph the wizard said to the crystal ball, "Oh crystal ball, show me the chosen one!" Sure enough, there was someone at a museum that appeared to be in a detective hat and coat. Ralph the wizard thought to himself, "That can't be him!" Ralph the wizard couldn't believe that could be the chosen one to save the universe. Suddenly, Ralph the wizard's friends were knocking at his door to ask if he had found the chosen one. Ralph the wizard said, "Yes I have, sort of, it seems like the chosen one that I saw in the crystal ball was wearing a detective hat and coat". Ralph the wizard's friends couldn't believe that could be the chosen one. Ralph the wizard and his friends were in deep discussion. Sophia the unicorn said "If he is in a detective hat and coat he can't be very powerful." Bentley the troll said, "This guy doesn't seem like he would be the type to defeat Carey the dragon and Doug the crow." The oatmeal warlock said, "How are we supposed to know if this person is worthy?" Ralph the wizard said

"Like I said before, you are all going to have to put him up to some sort of test because I don't know if this person has any potential". Ralph the wizard's friends headed back to their homes while Ralph the wizard asked himself how he was going to get to the chosen one's world. So, Ralph the wizard had to look through his books to see how he would teleport to the chosen ones world. However, he could not find any books on teleportation. He needed to go to the older library in the basement of his castle to find a way to teleport himself into the chosen one's world. Ralph the wizard grabbed a lantern and started to go into the deep dark basement. Even with the lantern, he was bumping into things because it was so dark. Ralph the wizard got to his old library in the basement and saw what looked like a very big book on a dusty shelf. So, Ralph the wizard took the old book off the dusty shelf and brought it upstairs to read. Ralph the wizard was looking through the book for hours and hours and hours because it was so big. Finally, Ralph the wizard came across something interesting. However, part of the page was missing. Ralph the wizard had to go back down to the basement to find part of the page that was missing from the book. Ralph the wizard was looking around the basement with his lantern. He searched the library from top to bottom to see if he could find the missing page. However, Ralph the wizard was having no luck. Then he noticed a piece of paper underneath a shelf. Ralph the wizard tried to grab the piece of paper, but it was stuck underneath the shelf. He needed to devise a plan to move the shelf. Ralph the wizard needed something that he could use to lift the shelf and he remembered that he had a dolly cart in his workshop. Ralph the wizard went back to his workshop to grab the dolly cart and took it to the basement to move the shelf. Ralph the wizard managed to move the shelf with the dolly cart. Sure enough, the paper underneath was indeed the missing page. Ralph the wizard went back upstairs to put the missing page into the book. Ralph the wizard found what he was looking for. Now he just needed to get his magic wand and open the portal. Ralph the wizard tried to open the portal but no luck! He went back to the book to make sure he was doing everything correctly, but again no luck! Ralph the wizard realized that he needed a potion to open the portal. He looked through his shelf full of potions to see which one he needed to open the portal. Ralph the wizard eventually found the potion he needed. He put the potion into a pot and started boiling it. Then, he used the potion, along with his magic wand to open up the portal. Ralph the wizard hopped into the portal and felt like he was going through a space warp hole which eventually took Ralph to what appeared to be a museum. Ralph the wizard saw a detective with a hat and a coat familiar to what he saw in the crystal ball! Ralph the wizard headed over to the detective and said, "My name is Ralph the wizard, I have a mystery in another world for you! Then the detective said, "My name is Detective Jon." Ralph the wizard said "This mystery is really critical, as it could mean the fate of the entire universe!" Detective Jon agreed to go with Ralph the wizard to the other world! Everyone else was "like are you crazy detective Jon?" Detective Jon said "Maybe I am or maybe I ain't!" So detective Jon and Ralph the wizard went through the portal to the other world! Everyone was amazed that they were gone!!

The End

Don't miss out!

Visit the website below and you can sign up to receive emails whenever Isaiah Fransen publishes a new book. There's no charge and no obligation.

https://books2read.com/r/B-A-KMEP-ICJJC

Connecting independent readers to independent writers.

Did you love *Before Jon*? Then you should read *Detective Jon The All 3 Books In 1 Collection Small Book Edition*[1] by Isaiah Fransen!

DETECTIVE JON THE ALL 3 BOOKS IN 1 COLLECTION SMALL BOOK EDITION[2]

Join Detective Jon In The All 3 Books In 1 Collection First Detective Jon Must Search For Sally's Missing Jewels And The Thief By Looking All Over Her Mansion After That Detective Jon Must Search For This Missing Artifact That Is Missing From A Museum And Track Down The Thief Finally Detective Jon Must Travel To The Hidden World As An Evil Dragon And Her Crow Are Planning To Take Over The Universe And It's Up To Detective Jon To Stop Them

---

1. https://books2read.com/u/bwr2Ve

2. https://books2read.com/u/bwr2Ve

Also by Isaiah Fransen

Detective Jon
Detective Jon And The Missing Jewels
Detective Jon And The Missing Artifact
Detective Jon And The Hidden World
Detective Jon The All 3 Books In 1 Collection Small Book Edition

Tasha The Last Princess Warrior
Tasha The Last Princess Warrior
Tasha The Last Princess Warrior Rise Of The Dark Princess Warrior
Tasha The Last Princess Warrior The Sorceress Of Power

Standalone
Before Tasha
Before Jon

About the Author

Isaiah who has autism resides in the beautiful Okanagan Valley which is situated in the Southern part of British Columbia, Canada. Taking in the latest movies at the local theaters is one of his favorite pass times. His interest in solving mysteries has lead to his desire to write about them. His books is full of exciting plots and adventures. Playing video games keeps him busy the majority of his time but finds time in his sometimes hectic schedule to write and looks forward to publishing more of his work.